PENELOPE GOES PARACHUTING

CARRIE PAINE

DEDICATION

This book is dedicated to my first friend, my sister Sue Sue.

She is never shy about telling the story of how I went to school
and told my classmates I went

parachuting with my grandfather. The Nuns of Sacred Heart
pulled her to the side and asked her

if it was true or not, over 58 years. But never again, because now
I have it in writing.

The front of school was filling up with all the friends after a fun spring break. Some critters' spring break was more fun than others. Well this is how Penelope felt.

"I will have to come up with a fun and interesting thing to tell my friends."

OH BOY...
NOW I NEED TO THINK OF A GOOD STORY TO TELL EVERYONE WHAT I DID OVER BREAK!

Buff walks over and says hello to Penelope.

"Penelope, did you have a good spring break? How did you spend your time away from school?"

Penelope just blurted out, "I went parachuting with me grandpappy"

Buff's eyes got very large and in disbelief he said, "REALLY"

Penelope quickly walked away so she had time to put the details together for her story.

The school bells' rang and all the students started entering the building. Timothy Toad yells out to Penelope, "hey if it isn't the flying Possum!"

ST ONES

Professor Bullfrog gave an inquisitive look, and asked Penelope why Timothy would say something like that to you.

Before Penelope stopped to think, she blurted out again,"I went parachuting with my Grandpappy."

The class erupted in chatter,each critter
curious about the event and Penelope

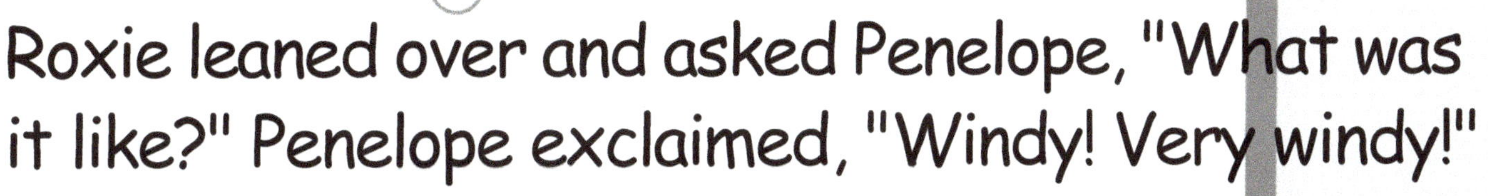

Roxie leaned over and asked Penelope, "What was it like?" Penelope exclaimed, "Windy! Very windy!"

Professor Bullfrog called the class to order and asked if anyone could share any new experiences they had during spring break?

Roxi Raccoon, told the story about her camping trip into the deep woods near a stream. Roxi caught fish and washed them on the shoreline.

They were very lucky because some humans left a ton of delieshes food behind in a barrow.

Professor thanked Roxi and then the classes started yelling out Penelope's name. They wanted to hear about Parachutting.

Penelope's face turns red and she knew she walked herself right into a box of problems.

Penelope started out by speaking about the lessons she and her grandpappy took. All her classmates didn't take their eyes off of her. She told them the parachute was three sizes bigger than her, but it was okay, she is strong and had no problem carrying the chute on her back.

SKYDIVING SCHOOL 101
A A A A A A A A A A A A H
STUDENT
STUDENT

Terrance raised his hand and said," weren't you scared?" As Terrance pulled his head further into his shell.

"No," said Penelope," In fact I needed to hold onto my Grandpappys hand because he was very scared."

Professor thanked Penelope for her story and asked her if she will be going parachuting again.

Penelope answered with a "No, my
Grandpappy, got too scared

That evening after school let out, Professor Bullfrog gives Mrs. Possum a call.

"Hello Mrs. Possum, this is Professor Bullfrog. I would like to ask you about a very dangerous activity Penelope said she participated in with her Grandpappy."

"What would that be" said Mrs. Possum.

"She did what!" exclaimed Mrs.Possum.

"Thank you Professor, I will have a talk with her tonight before bed."

The whole time Penelopy was peeking around the corner and heard the conversation. "Boy am I going to get into trouble!"

"Goodnight Mama", said Penelopy. "Wait"said Mama Possum, "I want to talk to you"

Here it comes, thought Penelopy.

"Penelopy, do you know what a white lie is?" "No",
Penelopy shook her head.

"Well it is a lie that hurts the one who tells it!"

"Penelopy, why did you tell your classmates you went parachuting with your grandpappy?"

"I didn't do anything over spring break and I wanted to show I had as much adventure or more than the other critters."

"Penelopy, there will always be someone who will have something you do not have and that is okay, because you will always have something someone else may not have." Mama Possum said in a soft and calm voice.

"Remember a lie is a lie, friends will stop believing you if you continue to tell these lies. You may even end up without friends."

"No friends!" Penelope said in a sad voice. "I want my friends, so I will tell them the truth tomorrow in school."

Mama Possum cuddled the blankets around Penelopy and said "always be happy for what you have and work hard to continue growing."

Penelope fell into a deep sleep. "No! No!" shouted Penelope as she slept.

RIBIT
00

Morning came fast and Penelopy was on a mission to tell the truth and apologies for telling a story that was a white lie. She said she wanted all of them for friends and promised to only tell the truth from this time forward.

HELLO MY FRIENDS!!

"About the Author"

Carrie is a person who wears many hats. She wears the hat of Daughter to parents that

encourage goals and reach for the stars. Carrie is also a wife and mother, along with being

a sister, and an aunt. She was born and raised in a beautiful city called Appleton

that is located along the Fox River in Wisconsin.

Carrie has always been interested in human behavior and brain development. She began

to see common behaviors in different age groups. She also saw how children developed

self character by having interaction with the adults in their lives. Her series, Buff and Friends

touch base on many somewhat common behaviors. This book Penelope touches base

on little white lies. This is the beginning phase of integrity and will grow with their brain

development. Children learn from examples, so please take the time to talk with your child

about behavior. Pointing out favorable behaviors.

Let's Reflect
You Tell Me

1. Why did Penelope feel like she had to tell a story?

2. Have you ever told a story that was not true?

3. Are you hurting anyone by telling a false story?

4. If your friend was Penelope, what advice would you give her?

5. Finish this old phrase:

HONESTY IS THE ______ ________.

THE END